Benny, the Bell Buoy

Written and Illustrated by Kevin Gabor

DEDICATION

This book is dedicated to my two grown children, Matthew and Emily. They have given me the greatest gift on earth in allowing me to be a dad. Through them, I have seen the love children have for the simple things in life.

Benny is a harbor bell buoy who spends his days floating at the entrance to a large harbor near a small town. He has an important job of making sure the boats entering and leaving the harbor stay in the deeper water and don't go into the shallow water.

Benny is painted bright orange so the boats can easily see him and he has an old brass bell that he will ring, DING DING...DING DING...with the rocking of the waves and if weather gets bad causing the waves to get bigger he will warn the boaters...DING DING...DING DING!

Every day, the boats would pass by Benny heading out to sea and he would smile at them and the boats would smile back at Benny.   There were cargo ships, yachts, sailboats and...

...his good friend Tippy the tugboat.

Benny was secured to the bottom of the harbor with a long, heavy chain and anchor so he didn't drift away because his job of keeping the ships and harbor safe was so very important.

But Benny always wondered what it was like out in the big ocean.

He had never left the safety of the harbor like all the boats and ships do.   Sometimes he would try to free himself by pulling hard on his chain and leave the harbor so he could head out to the big, blue ocean but he was stuck there, anchored in one spot.

Every couple of years a big boat called a "buoy tender" would come to pull Benny out of the water to shine his brass bell and clean off the barnacles and seaweed that would get attached to him.
Sometimes they would even give Benny a fresh coat of paint too.

One day, the buoy tender came and carefully picked Benny up out of the water and placed him on the deck of the ship and began to clean and paint him.

During the night, when all of the crewmen were asleep, the ship began to rock, back and forth...back and forth until Benny rolled off the ship and into the water "SPLASH"!! Benny floated away and out to sea he went.

In a short while, the only light Benny could see was the tiny light at the harbor shining from his friend Louie the lighthouse.

The next morning when the sun came up, Benny was all alone out in the deep blue water and all he could see was the ocean all around him.

Suddenly a large whale swam right up to Benny and made a loud SWOOSH as he blew water high into the air!

Soon, a friendly pelican came and landed right on top of Benny! The pelican thought sitting on top of Benny would be a great place to rest while he ate his lunch.

Benny loved the big, blue ocean and thought how wonderful it was to finally get to see it.

But Benny began to miss the harbor and all of his friends, he wanted to be back at the harbor entrance doing his old job of keeping the boats and harbor safe and ringing his bell as he rocked in the waves. Benny began to get very, very sad and even a little home sick too.

Benny looked up and saw something way off in the distance.

It's Tippy, the tugboat, out looking for Benny!! He's trying to find him; he's come to rescue Benny! Benny began to rock back and forth, as much as he could, until his bell began to ring. DING DING....DING DING!! He kept ringing his bell, hoping Tippy would hear him. DING DING.....DING DING!!! DING DING!! Louder and louder he got with each tilt he made. His bell got louder and louder and louder!!!

"There he is"!!! yelled Tippy's captain, "There's Benny"!!
The captain turned Tippy around and raced over to
Benny!
Tippy pulled up beside Benny and picked him up. They
carefully placed Benny on the deck, "Secure him tight, we
don't want to lose Benny again" the captain said.
They tied Benny securely to Tippy so he couldn't roll off
the deck. Tippy then headed back to the harbor and
placed Benny back in the water in his usual spot at the
harbor entrance.

Benny was SO happy to be back because he had missed the harbor and all his friends. He would no longer try to free himself by pulling on his anchor chain. Benny realized that he belonged in the harbor doing his important job of keeping the boats and harbor safe. He knew the harbor was his home and that is where he always wanted to stay!

ABOUT THE AUTHOR

Kevin lives in Chattanooga, TN with his wife, Stephanie. They have 2 grown children, Matthew and Emily and two beautiful granddaughters, Madelyn and Penelope. Kevin is a military veteran, with 10 years active duty service in the United States Air Force as a C-130 Flight Engineer, stationed in North Carolina.

Made in the USA
Lexington, KY
17 April 2016